CAN YOU FEEL IT?

Dr. Antara Majumdar

SGSH Publications

BIOGRAPHY

Dr Antara Majumdar was born in a Bengali family on 1st May 2000. She is an intern of bachelors of Dental Surgery of 2019 batch in Kalinga Institute of Dental Science. Her internship is going to be end soon and she will get her bachelor degree by the end of 2024. She always uses to think to write whatever she is thinking and feeling. So, in the 2nd pandemic of 2021, she started writing in a quality manner. This book contains different types of write-ups. All this write-ups have different themes. Some are based on depression, love, inspiration, romantic horror, some truth of life that everyone should follow or must realise. Aims of this book are that, from this book they will get a different concept and different point of view to about these topics about which are mentioned in this book. While reading this book they will be able to relate it in their life. Some of the people will get motivation and will be able to combat and move on. In the stories of this book, characters names and places are imaginary but based on life around her.

ACKNOWLEDGEMENT

I have tried to paint a few known characters around my real life with brush of imagination and colours of my feelings.

I am indebted to my friends, especially Divya Trivedi to giving me this opportunity to publish my solo book as well as her trust and guidance. I also want to thanks those peoples those who teach me nice lesions in my life though its harts.

I also need to thank my Dad and Mom who have been my inspirations throughout. A special acknowledgement goes to my Granny Mrs Nilima Majumder who always love and care me .

I wish to thank all those seniors , juniors and my friends who love to read my write-ups and encourage me.

Dialogues

1) Love
2) Unexpected reality
3) Care
4) Fare
5) Surprise
6) Hope
7) Relief
8) Earth
9) Fortune
10) The real fact that every boys must accept.

1. LOVE

Love is not that which fades with time.

Love is that which deepens with time.

2. UNEXPECTED REALITY

What is seen is not always true.

On the other hand

What is true is not always seen.

3.Care

Showing love and affection.

4.Fare

The more you try to escape from me, the more I will be closer to you and the more you try to understand me or solve me the further I will go from you.

5.Surprise

Sudden shock of special feeling happened unexpectedly.

6. Hope

Hope is that one lighted candle in a dark room that gives you light until that darkness is gone naturally.

7. Relief

The feeling of happiness and peace that we feel after overcoming a stressful or painful situation.

8. Earth

Largest theater created by god.

9.Fortune

Fortune play a major role in life whether it's about life partner or career or birth or death.

10. The real fact That every boys must Accept

Just like by marrying a girl no husband gets right to get godly respect from their wife.

In the same way, no boy's become men just by heaving good body build.

THOUGHTS

1) Fortune of birth.
2) Fortune of death.
3) Fortune in case of career.
4) Fortune in case of life partner.
5) Luck of life.
6) Relation between 'Life' and 'Drama perform at stage'.
7) Similarity and Difference between money and respect.
8) Broken heart are the strongest.
9) Difference between love and Relationship.
10) Right way of judging or understanding someone.
11) Right way to take the right decision when you are in a dilemma.
12) Helping other's doesn't mean to obey other's .
13) Temporary relationship can never be a true love.
14) Before falling for someone.
15) Feeling of true love.
16) Before accepting someone's proposal.
17) Varieties of love.
18) Love of One-sided lover.

19) Different types of eternal feelings.
20) Like.
21) Attraction.
22) Crush.
23) Addiction.
24) Infatuation.
25) Love
26) lust
27) Healthy Relationship.
28) Toxic relationship
29) Real Gentleman.
30) A true husband.

1. Fortune of Birth

It is not in anyone's hand that in which
family you will born,
Rich or poor,
Happy family or unhappy family.

It is not in your hand that whether you will
give birth to
a boy or girl,
a healthy child or a child with disorder or
genetic disease or a still born baby.

2. Fortune of death

It is not in your hand that you can escape from the date of your natural death.

If you are outside and have no enemy you can be die due to accident.

If you are frighten enough from your death and never step out from your house out of your fare then you can also die by heart attack during sleeping.

So don't loose your chance to take a risk or difficult step in your life to achieve a happy life or be pride.

But never be so much daring or fool to take such a risk in your life from where you have no way to save your life too.

3. Fortune in case of career

Some people who always give their full effort and are good enough to establish themselves in a field they want to be but just because every time such an obstacles arrived at their peak time of career that never let them have any single chance to prove themselves.

On the other hand

Their are also some people who are not so good enough to establish themselves in a field they want to be but just because every time a miracle happened or due to the absence such obstacle they get a chance to prove themselves or sometimes without giving enough effort , they achieve a good place in their career.

Sometimes it also happened that.

Some people who always good enough to establish themselves in a field they want to be and every time a miracle happened or due to the absence of such obstacle they get chance to prove themselves and achieve the best place in their career.

Those "miracles and obstacles "are the signs of "destiny" which allow or reject us from our career.

4. Fortune in case of Life partner

Their are some people who never let any chance to get into a relationship with the person they love.

Sometimes some of them get their love for lifetime as life partner and some never get their love till their death.

Sometimes it's also happens that to whom they hate the most become their love and sometimes the opposite happens too.

Sometimes people loose someone sometimes miracles happen too.

Sometimes it also happens that they have to marry a person whom they don't want to be when they already are in relationship with someone whom they love. Inspite of having a good relationship they get married to someone whom they never want to be. Which is also a game of fortune.

Always keep one thing in mind. "Partners are already decided by god for each and everyone for us", " Whose name is written in fortune , he\she will be the only one".

Then why so feelings of insecurity?

If he/she is in your fortune then they will have to be your and you to be of their. Your all try and their all try will be fail from your departure from each other.

5. LUCK OF LIFE

Sometimes luck of life make us feel that, " it is not a life it like a roller coaster ride", "The ride which make you feel to much hackle continuous until that stop by their own and if you try to stop that journey by your own then you will die but if you keep patience and complete that ride then you will be alive and quit feel as a victory . "

In the same way when life is full of unwanted suspense story, thriller drama and full of adventure then those people sometime get so much tired of that they give of from their life and end their life their but those people who keep patience and overcome those hackle in their life tactfully became the victory in their life.

But on the other hand roller coaster ride also have a dissimilarity in their life. That is in" roller coaster" ride you may know that that hackle is not will be their for so long but in " life " their is no time limit for that.

6. Relation between 'life' And 'drama performed at stage'

This world is the biggest stage
Birth is the entry time of the person to start to play their role.
Death is the departure time of that person from the stage "world".
God is itself the producer, director and editor of that drama known as life.
God send every one of us to play our role here.
We all have the duty to play our role in the biggest drama " life".

A person playing a role in the stag can't leave their role incomplete while performing, they can't leave the stage as per their wish in the continuation of the drama.

Like that

No one have the right to leave their role incomplete in this world as per their wish. When you are alive it means you have your role in this world till now. You don't have the right to suicide and end your role as per your wish.

7. Similarity and difference between money and respect.

Both are basic importance in humans' life which can be earned on the basis of qualification and behaviour.

All rich people are always known as respected people but all respected people are not rich.

To earn money qualification is more important than behaviour.

But

To earn respect behaviour is more important than qualification.
All rich people are not always respected by heart. Sometimes people show fake respect to them.

They are mainly respected due to their position in society for profession not because of what they are as a person.

But people with good behaviour are respected whole heartedly. They are mainly respected for what they are more than their position in society for their profession.

8. Broken heart are The strongest.

If you think that if you break someone's feelings further and further then one day they will become the weakest then you are absolutely wrong.

Because if you break glass and its broken pieces further and further then a stag will come when you can't broke it's pieces further because that pieces become unbrokenable.

In the same way if you break someone's feelings further and further then they also become unbrokenable and that make them strongest because your ill-treatment make them heartless, feelingless and increase their tolerance level so much that they became the strongest.

9. Difference between Love and relationship

Love - Love is such a feelings wish has no boundary. Love is always one-sided until both of them conface their feelings for each other.

Yes love can be one sided and pure. A true lover always ready to sacrifice for their love without any motive.

But

Relationship - Relationship is different from that of love. It always have a different rules than that of love though lovers after confacing to each other came into a relationship .

Relationship can never be one-sided. Relationship should be value by both and both have the duty to give priority to each other equally to continue their relation. Relationship always have motive to get priority or gifts or time. In relationship their is no world "sacrifice " because they always have the motive to get the same priority or move than that for what they have done. In relationship their is " compromise " inspite of "sacrifice ".

10. Right way of judging Understanding someone.

Don't judge people just by their deeds, to judge someone as innocent or guilty you have to imagine yourself in their situation in their circumstances and then think that what you will do in that situation. Only then you will realise that at that moment and that point of view the person whom you are judging is right or wrong. Moreover you will able to understand about what other people's are facing in their life and slowly slowly your habit of judging someone will convert into understanding someone and will get inspiration form others life too.

11. RIGHT WAY TO TAKE THE RIGHT DECISION WHEN YOU ARE IN DILEMMA.

When you are in such a dilemma that you are confused to what to do in that situation. Then the only way to take the right decision is when you put yourself in a 3 rd person's position. That time just think that you are a 3rd person who know your each and every matter. Then from that aspect think that what will be your advice to yourself from that 3 rd person point of view.

12. Helping other's doesn't Mean to obey other's.

Sometimes people don't realise the different between taking help and using others. Some peoples help other's so much that those help seeking peoples consider them as it is their duty of those people to obey them when they ask for it in the name of help. So when those people deny to help sometimes those help seeking peoples won't able to accept the reality that a person can also have the right to deny too as helping other's doesn't mean to obey them.

13. Temporary Relationship can never Be a true love.

If being in relationship we don't able to feel
free to talk to them,
If being in relationship we don't able to trust
our partners,
If being in relationship we don't able to
share everything of our life with each other,
If being in relationship we don't able feel the
beautiful feelings of the flow to fall for each
other,
If being in relationship we don't able to
imagine the beautiful future of togetherness,
Then what is the fact of being in
relationship.

If relationship is just to show-off your relationship status in social media, to get gift from your partner, to just spent free times with them by doing erotic chats then it is just temporary it's not love.

14. Before falling for someone.

Before falling for someone for their sweet words and sweet deeds to impress you and their words that they feel for you , Be ensure that do real they feel for you or you are just timepass to spent there free times or either a opinion. Be ensure at the beginning that do they genuinely feel for you or not. If you don't do so in the very beginning and fall for that person by trusting their words then after a long times of being in relationship all of a sudden when you will came to know the truth , the bitterly truth you will be broken in such a way that you will not able to trust yourself too.

15. Feeling of true love.

True love is a feelings that you started feel for someone without your consciousness.
You will not able to understand or recognise that when you started falling for someone.
You will feel something different for that person.
You will become too much happy for that persons for every small matter that you never fell for other's for their same did.
Some of their bad habits will not a matter for your to hate or dislike that person that once you hate those habits the most.
You will not able to focus on anything.
Every moment you will think about that person

16. Before accepting someone's proposal.

The one who dump their partner for you as because you are better their previous one though their was no serious issue in their previous relationship or neither they were mismatch couple then before accepting that person as your partner atleast for once remember that in future if that person get another one who is better than you they can also leave you for the new one for the same reason.

Because such person are never emotionally attached to anyone.
Their only motive in life is to take pleasure and utilizes someone.

17. Varieties of Love

Love have different varieties.
It can be a couple's love,
brother-sisters' love, parents-children love,
friend's love, teacher-students love and so
many.

All these relation of love are different from
each other, have their own different way to
express their feelings and they are also very
different from each other

But all these are love, though they have
different way to express their feelings and
different motive but at the end all these
bond taught us the same moral and same
point of view that what the true love is.

18. LOVE OF ONE-SIDED LOVER.

Love of one-sided lovers are pure, they fall in love, started feel for someone out of their consciousness. They can't even specified that when they started fall for that person.

Their love are soo pure that their only intention for their love to see happy. Though they will be broken from inside after knowing that the person they love, love someone else but still they only wish for their loved one to be happy inspite of wherever they are, with whom they are and in what situation.

They will never conface their feeling to their loved one if they understand that the person they love don't feel the same for them. It is not because of the fear of rejecting and to get insulted. It is because they don't want to loose that person in their life as they are soo special for them. They don't conface just because of the fear of loosing them. They think that if they conface, their loved one will misunderstand them and will make permanent detachment from them, and may not try to understand their pure feelings for them and may think that they can harm their love life if they reject them. But they will not understand a true lover will never harm to their loved one.

19. Different types of eternal feelings.

Like, attraction, crush, addiction,
infatuation and love.
All these feelings are so much similar to
each other that often we use to consider
all is feelings as love.

But reality is that, though all this feeling are
similar to each other but all are actually
different from each other.

Their feelings and meanings, all are
different from each other.

20. Like

To finding someone or something pleasant whether based on looks or behaviour. This is temporary and very week feeling. Cause someone can like any random person for curtain things.

21. Attraction

When a eternal feeling force a person to someone or something they like. This feelings is quite stronger than like but this is also a temporary and very much week feeling.

22. Crush

It is a combination feeling of like and attraction. Crush can turn into love or infatuation on the basis of pure feeling and timing it last for that wanted person. But maximum time proves as a temporary feeling. As because a person can have a so many crush in their life and it keeps on changing in their life time.

23. Addiction

It is such a feeling which make feel someone that, that person cannot leave without someone or something they crave for. A person can be addicted to many person on the basis of feeling positivity or behaviour or desire or love. Even infect a person can addicted to their friends a well on the basis of their important in their life. It is not necessary to that a person will be addicted to someone only in love.

24. INFATUATION

It is such a feeling that will make a person feel that they are in love but in reality they are not in love . In short infatuation is the mirage or hallucination of love. The different of it from love is in relationship a person will hart their partner out of limit but at the same time they will also addicted to her partner as well. The person will become totally obsessive and dominating to their partner. The person will want their partner for lifetime but at the same time they will also not have minimum trust or respect for their loved one. The person who is in infatuation believe that if their loved one can't be of them, they will not be able to be that person to be of someone else as well. In that case they don't even hesitate to harm their loved one, result in acid attack or murder.

25. Love

love is the purest feeling in the university. Love is all about care , respect, loyalty and honesty. The person who love someone will never hart to their loved one. If the person get angry on their loved one they may show their angry but to a curtain limit, they will never do anything out of limit in angry so to hart their loved on. The person who loved someone will not only get physically attached to their loved one rather they will attracted mentally and emotional to their loved one. The person in love will be hart if their loved one become of other but they will never get jealous or hart that person whom their loved one love. In love the person treat their loved one as priority not as a option nor as a toy.

26. Lust

Lust is such a feeling where a person get physically attached or addicted to a person whether their crush or a random person on the basis of their looks or the way that person fulfil their physical desire and sex fantasy in the way they dream or more than the way they dream for. In lust there is no emotional attachment no respect no loyalty no honesty. It is such a feeling where the partner's treat each other as toy to fulfil their desire.

27. Healthy Relationship

In a healthy relationship, partner's have trust and respect for each other. They are loyal, honest and caring for each other. In such relationship the partner's feel a good companionship then romanticism. In such a relationship there is always a perfect balance between emotional attachment, compatibility, love making and mental stability and feeling positivity. In such a relationship if there was a fight between them but non of them will extend the limit to deeply hart their loved on. In such a relationship non of them feel extreme insecurity which will make someone's life measurable. But in such a relationship it is also necessary that both of their frequency of the flow of love is matching with each other.

28. Toxic relationship

In such relationship a person will always feel hyper insecurity for their partner as because they never trust their partner. They will be dominating to their partner in each and every matter. They will become rude, aggressive and disrespectful. In some cases it has found that some person did this toxic things to their partner in case fear of loosing their loved one but in some case it has also found that those toxic people did such toxic behaviour to their partner as because they are cheater and that's why they don't trust other .

29. REAL GENTLEMAN

A real gentleman is a man who know how to respect a woman. A man who safeguard a woman, not those man who just left a woman or a girl in their bad times or in danger. A real gentleman is a man who leave in the motto that if they are committed to their loved one and feel that connection and commitment from his partner as well then they will marry their loved one. The man who will make his parent's convince to let him marry their loved one, in case if he is fail to convince them then also they will marry their loved one without their parents will and make their parents to accept their loved on as his wife and to accept their loved one as their family member with respect and love. They are those man, at the end of the day they will think of only of that one person he loved no matter with how many girls he casually flirt or have friendship. They are not those boys whose favourite game is to play with someone's feeling and use them just to fulfil their desire and when their desire get fulfilled they betray them by telling them that they were never in their life, and their was no relationship, no proposal it was only her imagination.

30. A TRUE HUSBAND

True husbands are those who respect, care and protect their wife for life time. For them their wife is the most wanted person in this world of full of beautiful peoples. They will stand by their wife if their parents treated his wife wrongly. They are those husbands who will make their parents feel that their is no difference between daughter and daughter- in -law . They are those husbands who will help their wife to get adjusted comfortably in new family as because when a girl marry a guy and came into a his family, for them their family environment and rules and regulations are totally new for them, they need a companionship from her husband to help her to get adjusted comfortably in her new family. They are those husbands who will make their wife to feel special everytime whether by his words, cheep or expensive or handmade gift or surprises or by making their wife feel their eternal whole hearted lovc for her. They are those husbands who will support and stand by his wife for her career as well.

QUOTES

1) Touch
2) Life
3) Broken heart
4) Red colour
5) Lesson of breakup
   And rejection.
6) Be conscious.
7) People's psychology
8) Beautifull
9) Human's character
10) The reason why
    Most of the people
    Won't be able to
    Continue their bond.
11) Anger and jealous
12) Beautiful togetherness
13) Life is so
    Mysterious and
    Unpredictable.
14) Fantasy.
15) Power of fantasy.
16) Peaceful sleep.
17) Judging.

1. Touch

If a person from your opposite gender whom you hate or consider as wrong person touch you formally (good touch) then also you will feel that it's a bad touch.

But

If a person of your opposite gender whom you like give you a bad touch then also you will feel that that's not a bad touch rather you will consider it as a good touch mostly as fulfilling desire or fantasy and well know as " love making " .

2. LIFE

Some people always wish to god make their life interesting by creating some stories in their life as they bored in their daily normal life.

On the other hand

Their are also some people whose life are full of stories with thrillers, politics and drama and this became the hackle. And wish to god for a normal life.

3. Broken heart

He made the beautiful and biggest castle in the
universe which was made of card that
suddenly disappear.
And push me down into the darkest world of sad and
depression.

4. Red colour

From colour of love to the sign of married women it
show the colour of true bondage of love.

From colour of blood to the sign of danger it show
the evil or death of someone.

5. Lesson of breakup and rejection

Never give too much priority to someone.
Never feel someone too much special if they won't value you or feel for you in return.

Otherwise you will loose your importance for them and they will take your feelings as taken for granted.

6. Be conscious

Don't give the key of your happiness in someone's hand who can't value you, who can't understand and never realise that how precious you are.
Once you do such mistake you will loose your happiness forever.

7. PEOPLES PSYCHOLOGY

A person will observe the character of another person in the way they actually think not in the way that person is actually is.

Means if a person is bad they will notice the bad character of another at first and if the person is good then they will notice the good character of another person at first.

8. BEAUTIFULL

Beautiful people's are not always good but good people's are always beautiful because of their beautiful spirit.

9. Human's character

Humans character is like dog tail.
Like you can't straight the curve of a dog tail in the same way humans character can't be change.

Human can change their behavior and habit but they can't change their character.

10. The reason Why most of the People won't be Able to continue Their bond.

People want you as the way they want your presence in their life,
not in the way what you are and also
not in the way you want to be in their life or you want them in your life.

11. ANGER AND JEALOUS

Anger and jealous are same kind of evil.

It not only destroys the person upon whom someone is doing so but also it destroy that person too who is doing so.

12. BEAUTIFULL TOGETHERNESS

Togetherness with the true person give birth to true bondage of love, who become the heart of each other which is inspirable and tends to feel beautiful feelings as beautiful as rose.

13. Life is so mysterious and unpredictable.

Some people whom you consider your life may become your strangers without any conflict.
And
Some who are stranger for you now will become the reason of your life.

14. Fantasy

There is no harm to fantasies spending beautiful moment's with the person they love but in reality they have no way to get them.
Their is no harm to fantasies some who don't feel the same for them .

But its harmful when they force their love to fulfil their fantasy against their will.

15. Power of fantasy

I love to fantasies you because atleast in there I able to get the happiness of togetherness.
In fantasy I am a successful person.
And this fantasy always give me the hope to struggle and tell me that yes I can do it and is the main reason to achieve those goal in real life.

16. Peaceful sleep

When someone cry unconditionally and as a result of exhaust by crying, they fall asleep.

17. Judging

No one has the right to judge someone only by listening from one party only.

But the sad reality of this world is that peoples do this mistake always.

Some special messages

1) Life is like a coin , it can
   Turn anytime.
2) Missions in life that
   Everyone must follow.
3) The rules of life.
4) The symptoms of love.
5) When loves walks away.
6) Night always long for.
7) You are like that star.
8) Special message for a
   Special person.

1. LIFE IS LIKE A COIN , IT CAN TURN ANYTIME

What is causing you to be happy today may be the reason for your extreme sad tomorrow.

The person whom you love more than the limit today, tomorrow you can hate and hate the same person so much that thinking about him can make you feel disgusted.

Those whom you trust today with your eyes closed, tomorrow they can become the reason to doubt others more than your limit and stop believe and trusting others.

The man who can teach you to live can teach you to die.

Who is your best friend today can be your worst enemy tomorrow.

Who gave his life for you one day may be the reason for your death tomorrow.

2. MISSIONS IN LIFE THAT EVERYONE MUST FOLLOW

To make, your parents proud.

Being soft, humble and friendly to everyone but never let your good behaviour to be your weakness.

To give priority to those who value you, understand you and never give up on you.

Never let a misconception and misunderstanding be the reason of breaking the strong eternal bondage with those true people of your life.

3. The Rules of life

Never lose your consciousness out of emotion.

Be soft from outside but be strong hearted.

Never take any step out of emotion.

Be grounded enough to accept reality.

Never give up your career by coming in someone's word.

Never believe anyone more than yourself.

4. The symptoms of love

When the absence of someone special for a few days make you feel so lonely like you are missing that person form so many years.

When someone understand your situation of heart although you try your best to hide it from that person.

When someone feel happy for your happiness and sad for your sadness.

When someone can do anything to be with you and to see you happy always.

5. When loves walks away

Love walks away when you disrespect them.

Love walks away when you try to control their life that deprived them to be happy anymore.

Love walks away when you cheat them.

Love walks away when you don't appolize or feel guilt inside for your wrong did.

Love walks away when you just use them for your own benefit.

Yes it happen.
If you don't rectify yourself within time.

6. Night always long for

Night always long for them who are enjoying
the whole night with love.

Night always long for them also who are
broken heart, crying the whole night by
hugging a pillow tightly.

Night always long for them who missing
someone every moment by losing them

Night always long for them also who can't wait
for their someone the "love".

7. YOU ARE LIKE THAT STAR

You are the star who show me the right way
when I am in dark.

You are the pole star of my life, who show me
the correct direction of that place where I
want to go.

You are the shooting star of my life, who
always make my wish true.

Yes it's you
You are the one.

8. Special message for a special person

I love the way you love me.
I love the way you understand me.
I love the way you are always there for me.
I love the way you always understand the truth behind my every lies.
I love the way you care for me.
I love the way you trust me.
I love the way you always understand what is going in my mind and heart just by seeing at my eyes.
I love the way you make me feel so special.
I love the way you came in my life and will be there always.

Poems

1) It's not easy for me to love you.

2) My sleepless night.

3) The window of my room knows everything.

1. It's not easy for me to love you.

It's not easy for me to love you,
When I was waiting for you to celebrate
our 1st anniversary ;
You were not there,
You were busy enjoying with others,
forgetting about the special day.

It's not easy for me to love,
During my difficult times, when I
needed you the most ;
You were not there,
You left me alone to struggle there,
So that the situation does not affect
your dignity.

It's not easy for me to love you,
When I always tried to understand you
blindly by listening your silly excuses,
but
You were not there,
You were never there to trust me for
anything, instead you always blamed me

for things which were never done by
me.

How can you expect love from me?
How can you expect it from me?

When relationship means to use
somebody to get benefits and instead
never give minimum respect to your
partner.

You have no right to expect love from
me.

It's not easy for me to love you,
But I tried it;
For a person who never deserved it.
And now it's not easy for me to love
you.
Because I cannot accept all these
anymore.

2. My sleepless night

At night, when I see the sky;
Hugging a pillow tightly, sleeping aside;
Recalling all those beautiful memories
we spent that time.
Suddenly I look at that empty side of
the bed, and imagining you there.
So many promises, So many plans;
which will come true those we made
that time.
I use to feel that, how lucky I am;
Yes how lucky I am to get you.
Oh yes! I was.
You were such a guy who always treated
me as a princess;
Loved me so much like no one else
use to do, and can never be like you.
You are love; you are the one for me;
Who save my life by giving his one.
Thinking those thought, tears fall down;
Oh my love! You are no more in this
world.
Looking through the window, talking
with those stars;

Request like a little child, to return
back my love.

3. THE WINDOW OF MY ROOM KNOWS EVERYTHING.

Oh my hubby! I call him.
Do you remember one thing, the
window of my room knows everything.
Oh yes! Our story.
From the day we saw each other for the
1st time.
Can you remember! It's that window
through which I saw you.
From your balcony you saw me,
looking at you in the way you fall for
me.
So many conversation so many letter's,
he use to pass for you to me.
"he! Who is he? "hubby asked me.
Oh! It's that window I am talking about,
I replied to him.
Oh yes! I remember ; Suddenly hubby
told me,
It's that window of your room your
parents caught us thieving.
"Thieving! thieving what? “I asked him.
Oh! Thieving each other's sole, my life.

"Oh yes! In the same way your parents caught us too doing so the other day. "I replied him.

We were so scared that time do you remember!

"Oh yes! How can I forgot" he replied to me.

We thought that they will never accept our relationship, as both of our family is against love marriage.

Utterly! The reverse happened;

It's a miracle or God's blessing I don't know.

"Our parents fixed our marriage without letting us know!".

Oh hubby! They still think that it's a arrange marriage, do you think so?

"I don't know! It's just you and me forever. "He reply so.

Stories

1. On my way back home.
   (romantic horror short story).
2. The raging story.
   (a tragedy).
3. To motivate a rape victim.
   (inspirational story).
4. The true bondage of love.
   (inspirational story).

1. On my way back home.

On my way back home, there is a beautiful solitaire pine forest.

Oh! the beautiful place to meet my love

Saying so I went inside. Setting beside by hugging each other, we confess our feelings, which we feel for each other. Suddenly I ask him, why everyone tell me, that we can never be together.

"No we will always be together ", he replied. Meeting my love after 5years, out of contact make me feel so deep in love. Looking at each other's eyes, expressing our eternal love. When we lost in each other's thoughts I don't remember. Suddenly I wake up it was dark then. I don't know when I slept. My love! Where are you? I exclaimed that time. Suddenly I found a grave beside me which was not there before. I was shocked when I saw the name and birth date written there. Yes it was no one, it's my love himself. And I faint there. When my sense came I found me in my bed. When I ask my father about my love he confesses me about his death.

He died in an accident 2 years ago which they hide from me.

2. THE RAGING STORY.

Sunny a polite, shy boy from her village went to Mumbai for her graduation in computer science engineering.

From his childhood he was kind and introvert and always stood top in his life whether is about any competition or exam.

Due to his shy and introvert behaviour he become the easy target of seniors as well as his batchmates too.

Due to his such shy character he has no friends no support. Everyone, even every girl used him for their notes or practical purpose by approaching him sweetly and after fulfil their motive they make joke on him or ragged him. So, being in a batch of 150 students , he was alone.

Before fresher's everyone had to face ragging. And he face the most shameful ragging, i.e., he have to stand necked in front of girls hostel for 10-11pm. He denied everyone and want an alternative but no one listen, not even faculty members as that senior was the son of principal.

He cried the whole night after standing naked as because many students taken his naked pic and make it viral in social media. But not only in this everything stop, after that incident he become the shame of that college and without any reason professors failed him under the instructions of principal as because he complained faculty against his son in case of ragging.

Being a son of poor father he become the burden, his father started blaming him by telling that he become that he is the curse of his life why he won't die.

At the end that pure hearted boy being alone and facing everything decided to suicide. So, he take a knife and went to college and infront of everyone he express his pain and point of view and end himself.

After that incident police came but due to lack of money Sunny's father don't case against any culprit of his son. And the case closed.

3. To motivate a rape victim.

Nisha is the 1st girl of 3rd year batch and the best student of Stephens Medical College. She is also the most discipline and hottest girl of that college, and that's the reason she is always the centre of attraction of every students as well as professors too.

Amit the professor of ENT department and biggest doner of that college. He is one of the most respectful person of that college.

But within students their is a bad rumour about him, i.e., " Many times he tried to molastrate many beautiful students of this college, and due to his fear and blackmailing those student left the college ". Nisha never use to believe her batchmates about that rumour about Amit and use to argue with them, coz she is also the centre of attraction of Amit too.

One day in ENT theory class in Amit class Nisha forgotten her mobile . It was the closing time of the college. So, Nisha also left with her friends. After going a certain distance she remember that she left her phone at college. So, she went back there.

Utterly Amit was present their alone, Nisha came, she greed him and as soon as she went inside to take her phone, Amit lock the door and rape her brutally. The busted! Why he will leave such a nice chance to take the pleasure of the hottest girl of that college.

After that he threatened her to not to disclose this incident otherwise he will lick her nude pic and MMS. Then he left the room.

Nisha quickly call Ritesh her bf the son of founder of that college for help. Luckily He is there in that college that day. She tell him the whole incident and sick him help to take the CCTV footage of that camera of that day. Ritesh do so immediately and came to Nisha to help her. At 1st he went her to another hospital and collects all the valuable evidence against Amit and then her treatment of her wounds. Doctor informs police this incident. They Arrest Amit but unlucky Amit lick her nude pic and MMS as he saw police came to arrest him.

Overnight Nisha become viral for those.

She and her parents become depressed as they belong from a conservative family. Nisha's uncle-aunty (Lali and Dev) came to their home. Lali went to Nisha, hug her and stop her from crying. Knowing everything she again asked her why she is sad. Nisha shocked, she replied she loose her virginity due to rape and her nude pic and MMS become viral overnight. Then Lali ask her that, " whether being raped is a guilty of girl or a boy? ". Nisha reply, "the boy that busted ". Lali then tell her, "don't guilt yourself then when it is not your fault ", and also say that

" Nisha it is 21st century, and in this early no-one judge any girl on the basis of their virginity, only narrow minded peoples do so. Now in this days many girls use to lose their virginity by doing one-night stand and sex with their bf and leaving a happy life like nothing happen. While losing virginity before marriage with their own will is not a crime in this era then why you feeling guilty for losing your virginity without your will. ". Then

Nisha ask and what about social media, I am viral girl now what about that. Then Lali tell her that nothing will happen now I stopped everything their but those who downloaded those are not in my hand but being your viral there is not the crime of only Amit. If those views of his social media wouldn't share those. All those who share that post are as guilt as Amit. But Nisha stop thinking about social media now because when a new attractive news and topic will come everyone will stop and forgotten the old topic. So, with the flow of time everyone will forgot you too, but now at this moment if you will struggle for your justice then you will be an inspiration for every victim like you. On the other side Dev was motivating Nisha's parent's in the same day.

Ritesh on the other hand found all those documents of those ex-students of that college who left the college in a mysterious way. He contact them and their parents and ask them to be the witness in this case to punished that Busted. All of them agree.

1st day of hearing arrived, Nisha having all the valuable incident and proper witness she win the case. While Amit can't able to buy any Nisha's witness by trying to giving them any compensation as because everyone of the witness are the victim of the same person.

Now, Nisha feeling herself strong, use to motivate others and is continuing her medical courses with confidence physically and mentally.

4. The true bondage of love.

Ria a sweet, humble, innocent and pure hearted girl of Ramesh Roe. Ramesh is one of the successful businessmen of India. For Ramesh Ria is her everything, she is his only child. After the death of Rita, his beloved wife after giving birth to Ria, Ramesh taken the responsibility of Ria. Before Rita's death he promised her that he will never many any another women and he will never let any reason for Ria's sadness. He will proved himself to be the best father. He always use to give Ria whatever she want and sometimes before she want those from him. He not only give him expensive gift but also he taught Ria a good behaviour and good attitude towards other.

Once Ramesh face economic crisis due to a failure of a business project in which he invested 20crore. But he never let Ria to know about it and inspite of facing so much crisis he continue to give her luxury life. Once Ria like a expansive dress, Ramesh don't have so much money that time to give her that expensive dress so he sell his blood in bank and brought that dress for her without let Ria know about it. Ria is the princess of Ramesh. After few month of that incident Ramesh overcome that economic crisis due to the successful of a business project where he had invested 20 lakh but done a profit of 20 crore. It is really a miracle happen.

Rahul, Ria's childhood best-friend. Rahul love Ria so much that he never let get hart Ria. He always use the Ria's unpaid bodyguard. When Ria forgotten to do or bring her homework in school, Rahul is the one who use to save Ria from getting punishment by giving his homework to her and punished by teacher. Rahul is also a black belt winner in karate. So he also save her many times from creepy people in school. He always use to support her mentally and psychologically.

Both of them have decided to get admitted in same collage in Mumbai but there, this childhood plan won't success. Ria get chance in St. Marry Collage in Mumbai and Rahul get chance in St. Stephen college in Delhi. From here they started their new phase of life. Ria become the centre of attraction in her college. She is the hottest, richest and sweetest girl of her college, not only that she is also a good student. Remo the son of funder of that college, the hottest, handsome guy, who is also a good student too and thus the centre of attraction of every girls of that college. Like other boys, Remo also have crush on Ria so once he propose her and she also accepted his proposal as she also have crush on him. Within a few days they stated to known as the perfect, romantic couple of that college.

First few years their relationship gone so well that Ria started forgetting Rahul. Their love life become so erotic and its going so well that they started live together. But Ria always use to ignore some matter in their relationship that he never paid bill of restaurant neither he every give any interest to meet Ria with his family. But after 3 years of relationship Remo started two timing with Ria. Remo's father fixed his marriage with CM's daughter, Rina. So, when Ria tell Remo about her pregnancy, Remo convinced her for abortion by telling her that he don't want to spoil their newly marriage life and if they have a baby in their newly marriage life then both of them will have to time for romance and spending time with each other. Ria love Remo so blindly that she get influenced by him and done her abortion. After her abortion when she asked Remo to marry her, she was shocked by his words and expressions. Remo laughed at her and her all the truth that he gets married with CM's daughter Rina. He tells her for abortion so that he don't want to face any problem in their marriage life. He also tell her that how he used Ria economically, physically and emotionally. He proposed her as because he was just physically attached with her and he make her fell emotionally by making her believe that he love her truly because he know that otherwise Ria will reject him and his dream of being physical with her will never come's true.

After she gets discharge from hospital she call Rahul and tell him to plan a friends trip in Darjeeling. Rahul planed it accordingly. They went to a resort which was located near the pic of a mountain. After having lunch Ria planned for the evening trip to go to the pick of the mountain to enjoy its view. So, all friends agreed and went for that trip. There are many stole of delicious street food. Ria and Rahul went to a stole which is quite fare from the cliff of that mountain from where they can enjoy the view. Ria from her childhood have a habit of dairy writing he use to write all incident of every day in it also what she felt. She also have a habit of caring her dairy with her everywhere which is only known by Rahul. On the other hand Rahul have a habit of reading her dairy in her absence. So, during this trip the same thing also happen. Once Ria keep her dairy in the that stole where she went with Rahul and tell Rahul that she is just went to other shop to see what she want to eat and tell Rahul to stay there until she return but forgotten to take her dairy from that shop. So, thus he get chance to read her dairy. But after reading it he was shocked and tensed for Ria and without wasting anytime she went in search of Ria but he won't found her in any stole and finally he decided to move towards cliff of the mountain as he doubt that she might can attend suicide.

On the other hand Ria at the solitaire cliff of the mountain, taking last few breath before ending her life. She closed her eyes and started thinking about all those beautiful memories she spent with Remo. Suddenly some questions stuck in her mind, what is true love? Do she ever felt it in her life? After a few moment of silence she got her answer that she never felt it was because the person whom he loved blindly just used him for his need whether physically, economically and emotionally. And ask herself that why she loved him? Thinking all those she felt anger and sad at a time and out of emotions she decided to jump. But luckily Rahul found her and pull her back before she end her life. Ria open her eyes, finding herself in her beastie's arms, she burst out with tiers. She sought at him by telling "Let me do it, let's end my life". "Why?" Rahul asked her. He again tell her "You should be happy, that you are now free from that toxic person". After a few moment of silence and observing her expression he again tell her " Oh dear! That beast never deserve a princess like you." Then with loud voice he asked her " How could you forgot , the bondage of love?". " Love ! " she exclaimed. Rahul then tell her " Yes, the love of we friends, the love of your dad" , " How can you be so selfish, how can you forget our sacrifice for you?" . Listening those Ria shocked, "

Sacrifice!" she exclaimed .Then Rahul tell her once, her dad shelled his blood to gift her expensive dress during his economic crisis due to business but he never let her know about it or felt it , and he , he always use to save her in each and every matter although he used to get bitten for that. Then he asked her " Doesn't our love have any value for you?" , "The person who never love you , and hart you ; you cried for him ! decided to end yourself." Listening those tiers fall down from her eyes . She thanks God by telling "Oh God! What I was going to do a moment ago?" . Then she tightly hugged him and confaced "Love you, thanks for realizing me the truth ".

www.ingramcontent.com/pod-product-compliance
Lightning Source LLC
LaVergne TN
LVHW010454160826
845677LV00012B/2489

* 9 7 8 9 7 9 8 8 0 1 6 5 5 *